Lily's Forest

PRAISE FOR *STORYSHARES*

"One of the brightest innovators and game-changers in the education industry."
– Forbes

"Your success in applying research-validated practices to promote literacy serves as a valuable model for other organizations seeking to create evidence-based literacy programs."

- Library of Congress

"We need powerful social and educational innovation, and Storyshares is breaking new ground. The organization addresses critical problems facing our students and teachers. I am excited about the strategies it brings to the collective work of making sure every student has an equal chance in life."
– Teach For America

"Around the world, this is one of the up-and-coming trailblazers changing the landscape of literacy and education."
- International Literacy Association

"It's the perfect idea. There's really nothing like this. I mean wow, this will be a wonderful experience for young people."   - Andrea Davis Pinkney, Executive Director, Scholastic

"Reading for meaning opens opportunities for a lifetime of learning. Providing emerging readers with engaging texts that are designed to offer both challenges and support for each individual will improve their lives for years to come. Storyshares is a wonderful start."
- David Rose, Co-founder of CAST & UDL

Lily's Forest

Mason Marino

STORYSHARES

Story Share, Inc.
New York. Boston. Philadelphia

Storyshares
Story Share, Inc.
24 N. Bryn Mawr Avenue #340
Bryn Mawr, PA 19010-3304
www.storyshares.org

Inspiring reading with a new kind of book.

Interest Level: Middle School
Grade Level Equivalent: 5.5

9798885977463

Book design by Storyshares

Printed in the United States of America

Storyshares Presents

1

There once was a forest on the edge of a city. It was deep and dark, with animals scurrying about in the undergrowth. Large trees towered overhead, dropping red and green treasures from their branches. Bears slumbered in their caves and deer pranced about in the tall grass.

The forest ran right up against a city. If you climbed a tall tree, you'd be able to spot the skyscrapers looming nearby. In that city, grownups warned children never to venture into the forest, and to always be wary of its dangers.

Being good children, most listened.

Lily didn't.

Lily lived with her family in the city, in a cramped apartment on the busiest intersection. Her parents worked hard to provide her with a good life, but this required them to have long shifts. Lily often had to walk by herself to school in the morning, passing by crowded storefronts filled with things she couldn't afford.

At school, Lily was quiet and reserved. The other children teased her for her shabby clothes. In order to escape, she would turn to her imagination, doodling small creatures that she made up in her head. Fantastical beasts, magical landscapes... anything she could dream up with would go down in her sketchbook.

After school was over, Lily would make the long trek back to her apartment to see if her parents had returned home. If they had, she would be faced with an afternoon of listening to them talk about grownup things. If they were not, she could sneak off to the one place where she felt she fully belonged: the forest.

2

The first time Lily went to the forest was purely by chance. Her apartment door had been locked when she had gotten home, so she decided to start wandering the streets. After a few hours she found herself right on the outskirts of the city, where only a few cars lingered and small, run-down homes remained. She wasn't allowed here. Her parents had always talked about how dangerous it was, but to Lily it seemed the same as anywhere else. The outskirts at least weren't as crowded as downtown.

It was as Lily was thinking about this that she saw a flash of green through a back alley. Green was a rare color in the city, the crayon in the bottom of the box at school that barely touched Lily's sketchbook. Seeing it anywhere, especially here in the outskirts, would surprise anyone.

Lily was a curious girl, so mustering her courage she walked through the alley and found... nothing. No streets, no cars, no noise. Just a wide expanse facing her, filled with trees.

Now, you have to understand that Lily was a young girl who had never seen much outside the city. Her family didn't make trips very often, and when they did, it was just to another side of the city to visit a distant relative. Lily had heard about forests and trees in her science classes, but hearing is much different from seeing. So it's no wonder that, being the curious child she was, Lily walked right out of that alley and into the forest.

It was love at first sight. Lily found herself facing a world that was new and unexplored. She played with small animals in the grass, she stole honey from bees and apples from trees, and of course she drew everything in sight. She added new colors to her drawings, ones she had never seen before in their natural states. Greens, reds, oranges, scenes of nature all filled her pages.

Her favorite things in all of the forest, however, were the deer. Some days she would just sit for hours and watch the herds of deer come by and graze in the tall grass. She saw how happy they were just to be around each other, and how they always made sure each member of the herd got the food they needed. Sure, they were just animals, but in a way it made Lily want those same kinds of relationships back in the city. So she started to participate in class.

She raised her hand more, and surprisingly had the answers. Her classmates who had seemed like people to avoid became friends she needed to make. Lily began to initiate conversations, and her classmates eventually began to respond.

Soon enough, she had her own little group of friends at school, who she even felt comfortable enough to share her sketchbook with. When they would ask her what the drawings were of, however, she kept quiet. She wanted to keep the forest to herself, her own little secret, just for a little while longer.

Lily's Forest

3

One day, after saying goodbye to her friends from school, Lily headed to find her favorite spot in the forest. In the heart of the forest there was a huge maple tree that shot right into the sky, complete with plenty of branches to lie back on.

As she headed to the tree, she daydreamed about all the things she wanted to do, like finally staying late enough to watch the stars come out above the trees. While she was thinking about this, she came upon the very spot she had been looking for and found just a single stump. No tree, no branches, no leaves falling upon your head. Just a flat stump.

The wind had been a little strong last night so it was possible the tree had fallen over, Lily reasoned, although she was disappointed that her favorite spot in the forest was now gone. She decided to go wait for the deer in the tall grass instead, but after an hour of waiting they never came. Now Lily was really puzzled. The deer always came to eat at this time of day. What could be stopping them?

Finally, a small deer poked its head out of the tall grass and began to graze. Smiling, Lily began to approach the gentle creature. The deer raised its head at her approach. But before Lily could lay a hand on it, it fell over, limp, an arrow sticking out of its side.

Suddenly, there was a huge group of men surrounding her with their loud voices.

"What are you doing here?" they asked.

"I could've shot you!" another exclaimed, clearly very worried.

Lily wasn't paying attention, though. She was staring at the deer that had been there just a moment before. How could they do that? The deer was just standing there. It wasn't hurting anyone. Not it lay dead on the ground.

The adults were looking at her now, urging her to get out. She uttered a protest in defense of the already dead deer, but they just yelled things she didn't understand about "contracts" and how she was "in the way of progress."

With tears welling in her eyes, Lily ran.

When Lily got home, she was surprised to see her mother and father already there, bags in hands. They sat Lily down and explained a new deal had been made at work, so they had received raises. This meant they had a little extra money and had decided to get her a gift from downtown.

"Now, Lily, we know the other kids at school have been teasing you about your clothing," her father said.

Lily perked up at this. The kids at school had actually been quite nice, but she would still be excited to have something to show off.

"So we decided to get you a new coat to wear! You're going to be the prettiest girl in school!" her mother exclaimed.

Excited, Lily dove into the bag to claim her prize. Dragging it out, she found her parents had purchased her a new deerskin coat. The image of the dead deer flashed before her. She dropped the coat in horror.

Beginning to cry again, Lily ran back to her room, much to her parents' confusion. She stayed there the rest of the day, the thought of the dead deer burned into her brain.

That night, her parents came into her room while she was trying to sleep. Looking up, Lily realized they had her sketchbook in their hands. Her mother sat down on her bed and began to stroke her hair. Her father explained to her that they had looked through her sketchbook and had seen the drawings of the forest.

They asked her if she had been going there after school. Lily told them, since there's no point in keeping a secret that's no longer yours.

Her parents were angry, but understanding, and simply forbade her from ever seeing the forest again. She was to head straight home after school, and if there was no one there she was to wait until the door was unlocked.

Lily began to cry, and although her parents tried to calm her down, nothing seemed to work. Eventually they both left her there, and she sat and cried for the forest the rest of the night.

4

After the men appeared in the forest, the city seemed to change. There was a certain buzz that Lily noticed as she walked to school every day. The storefronts were more full, their lines longer. The streets were more crowded than ever. There were more buildings popping up where there had been blank space.

Lily wondered if this was the "progress" the men had spoken of. If so, it seemed a crummy thing to lose a forest over.

At school, all the children had new things to bring to show and tell. Toys, clothes, pieces of candy, everything bright and shiny that a child could want seemed to be on display in the classroom.

Now, Lily also had these things. She found that people seemed to give her more attention than ever before. Even the teacher, a typically moody man, was in good spirits. Lily walked up to him one day and asked him to explain what "progress" looked like.

The teacher laughed and said, "Everything in this city is progress."

Lily was not very happy with this answer, so her teacher explained that progress was a good thing that made people happy, and that she was young so she needn't concern herself with it now. Walking home that day, Lily was left with more questions than answers.

* * *

Lily woke the next day with a sigh. Her life had felt dull and uninteresting ever since her forest had been invaded, and this day was no different. She took a look around her slightly bigger room, now complete with a window. Her parents had been able to move the family into an apartment one floor down with their new salaries. It was still quite small, but the windows were nice.

As she looked outside, she didn't notice the wisp of smoke coming just above the edge of the city. She began her daily walk to school. The streets were even more crowded than usual, filled with people who all seemed to be packing toward one of the city's many squares.

Walking behind the crowd, which was becoming quite noisy and agitated, Lily could hear a man near the front speaking. She heard him say, "nothing to worry about," at which the crowd began to roar with displeasure.

Over the noise it was hard to hear anything else, besides something about "new contracts" and "relocation." Quite confused about it all, Lily turned to a man beside her and asked what was going on.

"Didn't you hear? Everything's gone! The whole forest. Everything good we have in this city, we lost! What am I gonna tell my kids?" The man put his head in his hands and spoke no more.

Gone? The forest gone? No, this man must be mistaken. Her forest couldn't be gone. It was right there, right outside the city. Surely more people would be out here upset, outraged even.

Lily couldn't believe this, not without seeing it for herself. Pushing through the crowd, Lily ran towards the outskirts, running to find her forest.

5

Panting and out of breath, Lily ran through the back alley and burst out into where her forest should be. She found... nothing. No wide expanse of trees, no deer prancing, no tall grass. Just a few barren tree husks and charred ground.

Walking around this place she once called home, Lily found no signs of life. Some carcasses littered the ground, blackened skeletons of the creatures that once belonged here. Nothing else remained.

Lily didn't want to be here anymore. This wasn't the safe space she had come to love. This... this was death, this was despair, this was everything her young mind had been taught to be afraid of. She began to walk away, feeling dejected and hopeless. But when she got to the alley, she stopped and looked behind her one more time. As Lily stood there, right on the edge between the world she knew and the one she had loved, she made a decision.

She walked back into that diseased, dying place, and in it, saw beauty. Where there were burnt-out trees, she saw towering maples in her mind's eye. Towering maples with branches to lie on.

Where no grass stood, she saw a wide prairie where deer could graze. Where the ground lay blackened, she saw hills filled with flowers and fruit, where children of all shapes and sizes could play.

All around her, Lily saw a place that was beautiful once, and could be again.

So Lily went home. She went back to the city and started telling everyone she knew about the forest she loved, showing them the pictures from her sketchbook. Some listened. Some laughed and walked on. Others appreciated the pretty drawings and complimented her, but were far too busy to help her cause.

But some did help. It wasn't a lot, certainly not enough to replant an entire forest in a day. But every weekend, those same people came with seeds and tools in their hands and got to work in the dirt with Lily. And for her, that was enough.

There once was a forest on the edge of a city, and thanks to a brave little girl, one day there would be again.

About The Author

Mason Marino is a teen author from Virginia, USA. He has a strong connection with the environment and was inspired to tell this story to other teens to highlight the role that nature plays in our lives.

About The Publisher

Story Shares is a nonprofit focused on supporting the millions of teens and adults who struggle with reading by creating a new shelf in the library specifically for them. The ever-growing collection features content that is compelling and culturally relevant for teens and adults, yet still readable at a range of lower reading levels.

Story Shares generates content by engaging deeply with writers, bringing together a community to create this new kind of book. With more intriguing and approachable stories to choose from, the teens and adults who have fallen behind are improving their skills and beginning to discover the joy of reading. For more information, visit storyshares.org.

Easy to Read. Hard to Put Down.

Lily's Forest